Hide-and-Spook

Find out more spooky secrets about

Ghostville Elementary®

Ghostville Elementary®

Hide-and-Spook

by Marcia Thornton Jones
and
Debbie Dadey

illustrated by Jeremy Tugeau
cover illustration by Guy Francis

A
LITTLE APPLE
PAPERBACK

SCHOLASTIC INC.
New York   Toronto   London   Auckland   Sydney
Mexico City   New Delhi   Hong Kong   Buenos Aires

To Martha Levine — who is good
at everything — especially friendship!
— MTJ

To my wonderful neighbors Michael,
Stephanie, Brad, and Naomi Suinn,
and to the great kids at Leon,
Robinson, Garfield, and Ewalt
Elementary schools in Kansas
— DD

ISBN 0-439-56003-9

12 11 10 9 8 7 6 5 4 3 2 1   4 5 6 7 8 9/0

Printed in the U.S.A.   40
First printing, March 2004

Contents

THE LEGEND

*Sleepy Hollow Elementary School
Online Newspaper*

This Just In: Field Day Is on the Way!

Breaking News: Get your running shoes ready! Sleepy Hollow's annual Field Day is coming next Saturday. Lots of kids are busy practicing for the races. Andrew Potts is hoping to win all the third-grade events, but he'll have a lot of competition from the rest of his class. Personally, this reporter wonders if the third graders run so fast because they believe the school ghosts might be hot on their tails. Maybe that's how our school got the nickname Ghostville Elementary!

Tune in next time for more news.

Your friendly fifth-grade reporter,
Justin Thyme

1
Black Ribbons

"I'm good. I'm good," Nina sang to her best friend Cassidy. "I'm so good! Those girls didn't stand a chance against my volleyball team last night."

The two girls sat on the playground swings before school started. Nina wound her swing tighter and tighter. Then she let go and twirled around and around.

Cassidy leaned back in her swing until her curly blond hair touched the ground. She had tried to play volleyball in gym class, but the ball kept hitting her on the nose. "Did you win the game?" she asked Nina, even though Cassidy already knew the answer.

"Of course we won," Nina said. "We were awesome."

Cassidy pushed her swing higher. She had known Nina for years and Cassidy knew that Nina won whatever sport she played. "Congratulations," Cassidy muttered as she watched Jeff jog toward them. Jeff, Cassidy, and Nina had been best friends for ages. Usually they walked to school together, but today Jeff had overslept.

"Congratulate me, too," Jeff said. He pushed a ball cap down over his black hair before jumping on the jungle gym beside the girls. Unfortunately, Andrew wasn't far behind. If Jeff was one of Cassidy's best friends, Andrew was one of her worst. Andrew did pull-ups from a bar and stuck out his tongue at the girls. A little bit of Andrew's teasing went a long way.

"What did you do?" Nina asked Jeff. She chose to ignore Andrew.

Jeff grinned. "Nothing, yet. But I plan to win every race at the school's Field Day competitions next Saturday."

Cassidy wasn't the least bit surprised. If anyone could win races at Sleepy Hollow Elementary School's mini-Olympics, it was Jeff. He had the fastest feet in the school.

"Not if I win first," Andrew argued. "I've been eating my Wheaties so I can beat you."

Nina jumped off the swing. "I can't wait for the relay races. They're my favorite part of Field Day. They will be so much fun, won't they, Cassidy?"

Cassidy wasn't looking forward to Field Day at all. She wasn't particularly good at volleyball or running. And she was downright bad at catching and throwing. In fact, Cassidy was usually the last one chosen for teams during gym class. She wasn't the only one who knew it, either.

"Cassidy will probably earn black ribbons for coming in last at every event," Andrew said with a sneer.

"Cassidy is fast," Nina said before Cassidy could say a word.

"Yeah." Jeff nodded. "She's one of the fastest *thinkers* in our whole school," he pointed out. "She could beat you in a math relay any day."

Cassidy smiled, but she didn't really feel happy. In fact, she was feeling a bit left out and she had definitely had enough of Andrew. "I need to get my jacket," Cassidy said to Nina and Jeff. "I left it in the classroom yesterday and I'm cold." When Cassidy jumped off the swing, she stumbled and almost fell. Andrew laughed, but Cassidy ignored him.

Cassidy figured Jeff or Nina would come along with her, but they didn't offer. Cassidy sighed. At least she wouldn't have to listen to their bragging in the classroom. Sometimes Cassidy wished she could be good at running and jumping, but she'd never been all that interested in trying. She liked quiet better than all the screaming and noise that went with sports.

It was definitely quiet inside Sleepy

Hollow Elementary School. Cassidy's footsteps echoed on the stone steps that led down to her basement classroom. Cassidy pulled open the classroom door and took a step inside. Gloomy darkness swallowed her up. Their teacher wasn't there yet, so the lights were still out.

It took Cassidy's eyes a few minutes to adjust to the darkness. A chill ran down her back and she wondered why she had come into the creepy basement all by

herself. Then she remembered her jacket. It was lying across her desk. "There it is," Cassidy said to herself. Her voice echoed in the empty room. She reached out to pull her jacket off her desk when some-one or *something* grabbed her shoulder.

"Ahhhhhh!" Cassidy screamed.

2
A Sudden Chill

"Olivia!" Cassidy shrieked. "You scared the warts off me!"

Olivia laughed. "Now, that's something I've never done before." Her earrings jingled when she laughed, and the toolbelt around her waist jangled. Or maybe her toolbelt jingled and her earrings jangled.

Olivia had been the school janitor for as long as Cassidy could remember. She was known for saving homeless animals. Only, the animals she saved weren't always the kitty-cat and puppy dog variety. Today, Olivia had an opossum hanging from her forearm. As soon as the opossum saw Cassidy, it crawled into the pocket of Olivia's overalls and hid. Olivia shifted a package she was carrying from one hand to the other so the opossum would have more room.

Olivia chuckled. "Don't worry, Penelope is just feeling a little unsure of herself."

Cassidy wasn't worried about Penelope, but something else *was* making Cassidy uneasy. She had the distinct feeling that someone was watching her, and it gave Cassidy the creeps. She knew it wasn't Penelope, who was tucked away in Olivia's pocket.

Cassidy glanced over her shoulder. No one was there. When she turned back, she caught sight of the package Olivia was holding. A rash of goose bumps broke out on her arms. Something creepy was inside that bag.

Olivia noticed where Cassidy was staring. "I've been digging through old boxes," Olivia said. "And I've found many interesting things. Like this antique doll. Why, I bet she's been here since the turn of the century."

Olivia pulled back the paper sack so that Cassidy could get a good look at the doll. When she did, Cassidy nearly fell over. The doll's black eyes glared right at her.

Cassidy took a step back. Her day was getting worse and worse, and it had just started! First, she had to listen to her best friends brag about things she couldn't do, and now she was imagining that a doll was giving her the evil eye.

"What's wrong?" Olivia asked.

Cassidy didn't mean to tell Olivia anything, but she couldn't help herself. "Jeff is the fastest runner in our whole school," she blurted out. "And Nina is good at practically every sport. I'm not good at anything!" Cassidy felt silly for acting like such a baby.

Olivia jingled and jangled. "You're awfully young to worry about such things," she said. "The important thing is for you to find something that *you* like to do."

"Well, I am the best in our class at

using computers," Cassidy said with a nod toward the computers in the back of the room. Cassidy was already starting to feel better. After all, she was far ahead of the other kids in every computer game or skill they had tried in class.

"Now, that's something I've never tried," Olivia admitted.

"Oh, you should," Cassidy told her. "Computers can help in so many ways."

"My lands, why would I ever need to use a computer?" Olivia asked.

Cassidy had all sorts of reasons. "You could find out about new cleaning products and order them cheaper than you can buy them in a store. You could also find out how to take care of all different kinds of animals."

Now it was Olivia's turn to be quiet. The smile faded from her face. Even Penelope seemed sad when she peeked out of Olivia's pocket.

"Jumping jelly beans!" Olivia exclaimed. "I had no idea I was missing out on so much by not knowing how to use one of those contraptions."

"I . . . I could teach you about computers," Cassidy suggested.

Olivia perked up, and so did the opossum. "That would be right nice of you. I'll look forward to it."

After Olivia jingled and jangled out of the room, Cassidy felt a sudden chill. The air around her swirled with green flakes of glitter. Cassidy knew what that meant. Ghosts were on their way.

Ever since she could remember, Cassidy had heard rumors about ghosts haunting the boarded-up basement of her school. That's why the nickname Ghostville Elementary had stuck. It wasn't until her class had been moved to the basement that Cassidy found out the rumors weren't rumors at all. They were the truth. She had seen the ghosts with her very own eyes. So had Jeff and Nina.

Cassidy took a deep breath and prepared to face a classroom full of ghosts.

3
Ghost Tutor

The air turned so cold in the classroom that Cassidy had to button her jacket. Glittering flakes tumbled and twisted around her until they grew thicker and took shape. One, two, three green clouds turned into the shimmering images of kids . . . ghost kids. Cassidy knew who they were. These ghosts had been pestering her and her friends since the beginning of the school year.

Ozzy's dark hair stuck straight up and his sister Becky's long curly hair floated in the air around her head. Their friend Sadie floated off to the side. She looked like the saddest ghost in the world.

One, two, three more clouds bubbled and thickened until Cassidy recognized them, too. Nate, Edgar, and Calliope appeared. Nate was the tallest and quietest ghost. Edgar wore a tie and glasses while Calliope carried her violin with her. The group of ghosts hovered around the computers in the back of the room.

Two more ghostly shapes darted around the room so fast the green glitter stretched out like a cloud. Cassidy knew they were Ozzy's dog, Huxley, and Cocomo, Calliope's mysterious black ghost cat.

Cassidy automatically took a step back from the ghostly crew. No matter how many times she saw the ghosts appear, Cassidy knew she would never get used to it.

"So *that*'s what that box is," Ozzy said before the rest of the ghosts could say a word. Ozzy did somersaults through the air until he hovered right over Cassidy's head. "How do you make it work?"

Becky crossed her arms in front of her chest and stuck out her chin. "I've seen

you sit and stare at it for hours," she said to Cassidy. "It looks as boring as watching cornstalks grow."

Without thinking, Cassidy made her way to the back of the room and sat down at one of the computer tables. She tried to imagine what it would be like to live in the 1800s without computers,

but it was too hard. The ghosts tumbled through the air after her. "Computers are not boring," she said. "You can learn anything using a computer."

"Can I learn about writing stories?" Edgar wanted to know as he hovered above Cassidy's chair. Edgar liked to write the kind of stories that gave kids nightmares. In fact, Edgar usually spent his time inside a picture that hung on the classroom wall. He sat beside a tree and wrote in his journal all day long.

"Muuuuuu-sic?" Calliope asked as she perched on top of the computer monitor with her violin under her chin. "Will it play muuuu-sic?" Before Cassidy could answer, Calliope ran her finger across a string. The notes from the ghostly violin sounded like an owl with a sore throat.

Sadie moaned and floated off to the side. "Muuuusssic."

Nate didn't say a word. His spooky silence bothered Cassidy. She wondered what he was thinking as he peered over her shoulder.

The only ghost that wasn't interested in the computer was Becky. Becky was the youngest of the ghosts, but that didn't make her the least bit shy. "I don't want to sit and think," she said. "I'd rather swirl and dance!"

To prove her point she flew through the air, then twirled once before disappearing through a wall. Cassidy had learned that ghosts had to concentrate very hard or they would go right through solid things. Becky had a habit of not concentrating.

"You can learn all those things, but I don't think me being a computer tutor to ghosts is a good idea," Cassidy said. "After all, ghosts really shouldn't surf the Internet. They might get lost in cyberspace."

"Pleeeeeeaaaaaase?" Sadie begged as she flew toward Cassidy.

Cassidy jumped up from the chair and stepped out of the way of the flying ghost. The computer hiccuped as Sadie passed through it.

"No." Cassidy closed her eyes and shook her head. "No, no, no! I'll teach Olivia, but I won't share this computer with ghosts!"

When Cassidy opened her eyes, she found herself face-to-face with Ozzy, Edgar, and Calliope. Their eyeballs had grown to the size of oranges and not one of them blinked. Step-by-step, Cassidy backed up until she was flat against a

wall. With each step, the ghosts oozed through the air until they were within inches of her nose.

"We will learn," Ozzy said. When he spoke, Cassidy felt cold air rushing all around her, seeping down into her bones. "Nothing will stop us! NOTHING!"

4
Finkle's Deal

Cassidy was still shivering when the rest of her class filed into the room. "Are you okay?" Nina asked.

"You look a little pale," Jeff added.

"Thinking about losing every Field Day race has her scared," Andrew said.

"She's not going to lose every race," Jeff said.

"Yes, she will," Andrew said. "And I can prove it at recess."

"How?" Nina asked.

Andrew faced Cassidy and put his hands on his hips. "I challenge Cassidy to a fifty-yard dash!"

When Cassidy didn't answer, Andrew laughed out loud. "What's the matter? Are you afraid that I'll skunk you?"

Nina stepped between Cassidy and

Andrew. "There's a skunk around here, all right. And it's you! Cassidy's probably feeling sick because she smells your stinky feet!" Nina told Andrew.

"Oh, yeah?" Andrew asked, taking a step toward Nina.

A girl from their class named Carla walked past and frowned at Andrew and Nina. "Cassidy probably is sick."

"Sick of listening to you two argue," Darla, her twin sister, added.

"I know *we* are," Carla said.

Their teacher hurried into the classroom. "There you are," Mr. Morton said as if he had been looking for his students for an hour. "Sit, sit, sit! We have a busy day ahead of us."

The kids hurried to their seats and pulled out paper and pencils. All morning, Cassidy tried to concentrate on her work, which was very hard to do considering she kept seeing the air around the computers glitter and glow. She had heard of things called computer viruses, but she

could not imagine what would happen if the classroom computers got infected by ghosts.

Andrew didn't help matters. "Loser," he whispered every time he passed by Cassidy's desk. Cassidy knew he would be even worse on the playground. As the clock swept closer and closer to recess time, Cassidy's stomach churned more and more. She would have gladly faced a gaggle of ghosts just to avoid dealing with Andrew at recess.

As the rest of the kids lined up at the door leading to the playground, Cassidy went up to Mr. Morton's desk. "Excuse me?" she asked. "Can I ask you a question?"

Her teacher wiped chalk dust away from his glasses to look at her. "What do you want, Miss Logan?"

"Olivia doesn't know how to use computers," Cassidy said. "I thought I could help her during recess."

Mr. Morton scratched his earlobe. "But

then you'd miss running and kicking and all those fun things," Mr. Morton said.

That was the point, Cassidy thought to herself, but she knew better than to say it out loud. Instead, she nodded. "It won't be forever," she told him.

"This is a decision best made by the principal," Mr. Morton said. "Why don't you ask her?"

Cassidy waved to Nina and Jeff as they went out the playground door. Then Cassidy hurried up the basement steps. The rest of the school was bright with big windows and looked very new compared to the basement. That's because the brand-new school had been built over the basement of a one-room school-house.

The secretary waved Cassidy into the principal's office. Ms. Finkle sat at her desk and tapped her long painted fingernails on the ink blotter as she thought. "I'm not so sure it's a good idea to have you spend recess inside. After all, you

MS. FINKLE
PRINCIPAL

should be out in the fresh air. You should be running and playing. You should be kicking balls."

Cassidy cringed with every argument. She didn't feel like running and kicking, and she definitely didn't want to accept Andrew's challenge.

Then Ms. Finkle leaned across her cluttered desk. Her daggerlike fingernails waved in the air. "Besides, most kiddos would not feel . . . shall we say . . . comfortable in the basement with the rest of the class gone," she said. She smiled mysteriously before laughing a witchlike cackle.

Cassidy knew all the kids had heard the legends about the haunted basement. That is, after all, why they nicknamed their school Ghostville Elementary. But she didn't know how much Ms. Finkle knew.

"Why not?" Cassidy asked in her most innocent voice.

Ms. Finkle narrowed her eyes as if she

was thinking about telling Cassidy a big secret. Finally, the principal nodded. "I'll make you a deal. You may show Olivia a few things about the computer as long as you agree to participate in the upcoming Field Day," Ms. Finkle said.

Cassidy's mouth dropped open. She had planned on pretending to be sick that day. "But . . ."

"No ifs, ands, or buts about it," Ms. Finkle said. "I've made my decision! Is it a deal?"

Cassidy didn't know what was worse: dealing with a classroom full of ghosts or running a relay against Andrew. She did know one thing.

Cassidy didn't have a choice.

5
Techno-Gizmo

"Zip-pe-de-do-daw!" Jeff shouted as he leaped out of his chair the next day. "Recess time is perfect time!"

Nina smiled as she followed Jeff to the door where the whole classroom of kids had lined up — everyone except Cassidy. Cassidy sat at her desk with her hands folded.

"What's wrong with you?" Andrew asked. "Are you scared I'll beat the pants off you?"

"You couldn't scare the diapers off a baby," Cassidy snapped at Andrew. She was getting very tired of his teasing.

"Cassidy is being nice and helping someone at recess," Nina said walking over to stand beside her friend. "You should try being nice once in a while."

Andrew rolled his eyes. "I'd rather try beating you in a fifty-yard dash."

"You're on," Nina said as the kids raced out the playground door.

After the rest of the class left, the room became deathly still. Cassidy wondered if she had made a big mistake staying inside all by herself. She gulped as the door squeaked open.

Thankfully, it was Olivia and Penelope. Both Olivia and the opossum smiled. Actually, Penelope's smile looked more like a snarl, so Cassidy took a giant step back.

"Let's get this show on the road," Olivia said with a jingle and a jangle of her long dangling earrings.

"Okay," Cassidy said with a deep breath. "This is a computer." She sat down in front of one of the classroom computers and turned it on. When the computer screen sprang to life, Penelope did a little dance on Olivia's shoulder.

"Look," Cassidy said as she connected to the Internet to show Olivia a Web site about animals. "Here's everything you need to know about opossums."

"Good heavens!" Olivia said, putting her hand over her heart. "This is extraordinary."

Cassidy nodded, but there was something else she thought was even more amazing. Flying above the computer were green blurry images of ghosts.

Cassidy closed her eyes. What would happen if Olivia saw the green blobs?

Cassidy shouldn't have worried, because Olivia never took her eyes off the computer screen.

Edgar sat on top of the monitor and whispered in Cassidy's ear, asking for ghost-story sites while Nate politely asked to see sites about fishing holes. Ozzy demanded jokes. Sadie and Calliope wanted to learn more about music. Only Becky kept quiet.

Olivia smiled at Cassidy. "You're really great at this techno-gizmo stuff. It's almost as if you can see what I need to learn."

Cassidy shrugged, although she did like the praise. It felt nice to be good at something.

Olivia's eyes lit up. "I want to give you a gift for helping me and I know the perfect thing." Olivia rushed from the room with the opossum clinging to her shoulder.

Cassidy hadn't really expected a reward for helping. She wondered what

Olivia could possibly have in mind. Cassidy also wondered how in the world she could get rid of the ghosts that were floating around the computer keyboard.

Cassidy didn't have to wonder for long. The minute Olivia walked back through the door, Becky let out a bone-chilling scream that only Cassidy could hear.

6
Olivia's Present

"What's going on?" Cassidy asked as all the ghosts zipped out of the class-room screeching.

Olivia held out the doll she'd had the other day. "I want you to have this. Her name is Hilda," Olivia said.

The doll looked ordinary enough to Cassidy. It was old and dressed like a girl from the 1800s. But something about the doll's eyes bothered Cassidy. When she took the doll from Olivia, tingles ran up and down Cassidy's arms and her whole body got as cold as a frozen slushy. No matter how Cassidy held the doll, the eyes stared at her. Maybe that was what had scared the ghosts. She tried to give the doll back. "Oh, Olivia, I can't take this," Cassidy said. "But thank you anyway."

Olivia smiled and shook her head. Her earrings jingled or maybe they jangled. "It's yours now," she answered, "for better or for worse."

"Thank you," Cassidy said, even though she didn't want the present.

Cassidy put the doll on her desk and tried to forget about it while she taught Olivia more about computers. But when the class came in from recess, Andrew didn't waste any time teasing Cassidy.

"Cassidy plays with baby dolls," Andrew taunted.

"You *are* a baby," Cassidy snapped as she tried to stuff the doll in her desk.

Cassidy wasn't quick enough. Their teacher, Mr. Morton, saw the doll and ran right over to Cassidy. "Why, that doll is dressed just like someone from the 1800s," he said. "Would you consider putting the doll on display in our classroom? It fits right into our 1800s theme."

"Sure," Cassidy answered with a shrug. "Its name is Hilda." The kids had all worked to decorate their room like a classroom out of history. Cassidy had to admit the doll fit right in. She was glad to get rid of it. She put the doll beside the old coal stove the kids used to store their markers and crayons.

"All right," Mr. Morton said. "Everyone line up in the hallway next to the water fountain to get a drink. Then we'll get busy on our spelling lesson." The kids squeezed through the door and into the hallway. Andrew kept trying to cut in line, but Jeff and Nina elbowed him back to his place.

Cassidy was joking with Jeff and Nina as they came back into the room. The smile was wiped from Cassidy's face when she noticed Hilda was no longer beside the old stove. Instead, the doll was sitting on top of Cassidy's desk.

"What's wrong?" Nina whispered.

Cassidy pointed to the doll and gulped. "How did it get back on my desk?" she asked.

Nina rolled her eyes. "That Andrew. He is such a pest. He's just trying to make you mad."

"Maybe the doll moved on its own," Jeff said, his eyes getting big. "I saw a movie once where a puppet moved around."

"It *is* freezing cold when you touch it," Cassidy said, her voice trembling just a little, "like it's a ghost or something."

Nina shuddered, then shook her head. "No, dolls can't be haunted. They're cute

and cuddly." The three kids stared at the doll. It definitely didn't look cute or cuddly.

"Olivia gave it to you," Jeff said. "She wouldn't give you something bad, would she?"

Nina moved out of Carla and Darla's way as they came back from getting a drink. "You guys are being silly," Nina whispered to Jeff and Cassidy. "Andrew must have moved the doll. He did it to tease you."

Cassidy shook her head and pulled Jeff and Nina aside as the rest of the kids filed back into the classroom. "I don't think this is the work of Andrew," Cassidy said. "I think that doll is haunted!"

Nina giggled. "A doll can't be haunted."

"Why not?" Cassidy asked. "Houses are haunted. Why not dolls?"

"They just can't be haunted," Nina said firmly. "Dolls are sweet and innocent toys."

Jeff shook his head. "That's not exactly

true. In a movie I saw, the doll played nasty tricks on people."

Cassidy gulped again and peered at the doll. It stared right back at her. Cassidy had a horrible feeling that tricks were exactly what Hilda had in mind.

7
Hocus-Pocus

The next morning, Jeff, Nina, and Cassidy met in the classroom before school started. A cloud of dust floated in the weak sunlight struggling through the dirty classroom windows. A new cobweb stretched from Mr. Morton's desk to the file cabinet. The air smelled a bit like dirty socks. But none of that bothered Cassidy.

"Are you okay?" Jeff asked. "Did you see a new ghost?"

Cassidy shook her head. She opened her mouth to speak, but no noise came out. Instead, she pointed to her desk. There, sitting in her seat, was Hilda, and it was looking straight at her.

"Andrew is teasing you again," Nina said.

When Cassidy finally spoke, her voice squeaked. "It's not Andrew," she said. "I hid that doll in the coat closet after Andrew left yesterday."

"Then he sneaked in later," Jeff said. "This time, we just have to hide the doll someplace Andrew will never think to look."

Before Cassidy could say *hocus-pocus*, Jeff had snatched the doll and carried it to the hallway. Nina and Cassidy fol-

lowed him down the hall. "Andrew will never think to look here," Jeff said as he opened a storage closet and stuffed Hilda behind a box.

As soon as the kids closed the closet door, the air in the hallway turned so cold they could see their breath. A green cloud of glitter swirled around their heads. That could mean only one thing. The ghosts were back.

Ozzy and Becky popped in front of them. Ozzy peered over their heads. Becky looked around their backs. "Is she gone?" Becky asked.

"Good riddance, I say," Ozzy said.

"Who?" Nina asked.

"You know who," Becky said. She pointed a finger at Cassidy and sniffed. "You better be careful, that's all I have to say."

"She's right," Ozzy added. "With *her* around, there's bound to be nothing but trouble."

And then Ozzy and Becky disappeared like bubbles popping.

"What was that all about?" Jeff asked.

"Who were they talking about?" Nina wanted to know.

Cassidy didn't say a word. She had a terrible feeling she knew exactly who they were talking about. And if the ghosts were afraid of Hilda, then she knew one thing was sure: They should all be afraid. Very afraid.

Mr. Morton didn't give the kids time to think about the doll. He rushed down the steps and called, "Hop to it. There's much to do, so let's get busy, busy, busy."

Cassidy hurried back into the classroom and concentrated on a story she was writing. She chewed on the end of her pencil. Writing was not her favorite thing to do. She wished Edgar could help her. She looked around. No ghosts. But she did see something else. The doll. Hilda sat on the bookshelf right by her desk. Cassidy yelped. She couldn't help it.

"What's wrong?" Nina asked.

Cassidy pointed. Unfortunately, Andrew saw her. "Cassidy's playing with dolls again," he yelled out so the entire class could hear.

Mr. Morton wiped the chalk dust from his glasses and peered at Cassidy. "No time for playing," he said. "Work, work, work! Cassidy, please put the doll where it won't distract you."

Cassidy tried not to shiver as she reached out to grab the doll, but the mere touch of it turned her blood to ice. Cassidy held the doll far away from her body as she carried it to the coat closet at the back of the room. She buried Hilda in the lost-and-found box.

When she got back to her seat, Cassidy's paper was not on her desk. She looked on the floor. She looked under her chair. She looked inside her desk.

"Cassidy doesn't have her work," Andrew called out.

Mr. Morton looked at Cassidy again. Then he tapped his watch. "Time's a-wasting, Miss Logan," he said. "Better get busy."

Cassidy stuck out her tongue at Andrew before getting a new piece of pa-  per from her desk. She thought the doll was gone. No such luck.

After lunch, Cassidy found the doll under her seat. She wanted to kick it across the room. Instead, she carefully picked up Hilda by the gingham dress and stuffed the doll behind the bookshelf. She wiped her hands, sure that no one would think to look there. She was wrong.

The next morning, when Cassidy opened her old-fashioned desk, there, staring straight up at her, was Hilda. Cassidy almost screamed but stopped just in time. "This is getting ridiculous," she muttered. Every time she opened her desk, the doll looked up at her with a mean grin plastered on its china face. As soon as Mr. Morton gave the class a break, Cassidy hurried to cram the doll into the bottom drawer of Mr. Morton's file cabinet.

By the end of the day, Cassidy had almost forgotten about Hilda. The entire day went by without the doll appearing a single time. But when Cassidy opened her backpack, there it was.

By Thursday, Cassidy was past being scared. She was mad. "I can't take it anymore," she finally told Nina and Jeff as they got their backpacks to go home.

"That doll is driving me crazy. It keeps coming back to haunt me, no matter how hard I try to hide it."

"It's not the doll," Nina said.

"It's Andrew," Jeff said with a nod.

"You're wrong," Cassidy told them. "That doll is haunted. And I have a feeling it's going to cause trouble. Not even the ghosts of Ghostville Elementary want to be in the same room with Hilda."

"Cassidy has a point," Nina said. "Ever

since the doll showed up, the ghosts have made themselves scarce."

Jeff grinned. "Who would've guessed that a doll would end up being the one thing that keeps the ghosts away? We should be glad. This doll is the answer to all our problems."

"I wouldn't be worried if I thought the doll was harmless," Cassidy said. "But I don't think Hilda is harmless. Not at all!"

Nina looked worried. "You're being silly," she said. "I'm sure it's just Andrew."

"That doesn't make me feel one bit better," Cassidy said. "I can't win races. I can't play volleyball. I can't even hide a stupid doll from Andrew. I can't do ANYTHING right!"

"That's not true," Jeff said.

"You're good at plenty of things," Nina added.

"Name one thing," Cassidy sputtered.

Cassidy looked at Nina. She looked at Jeff. They were thinking and they were thinking hard. But they weren't thinking fast enough. "Just as I thought," Cassidy said. "You can't name a single thing."

Cassidy stormed out of the classroom. Nina and Jeff didn't try to stop her.

8
Gotcha!

As soon as Cassidy walked into the classroom on Friday, she looked for the doll. She expected to see Hilda staring straight back at her, even though she had hidden the doll in a bag of art supplies.

Cassidy looked around her desk. She looked on the shelves. Then she looked in the bag of scrap paper where she had hidden Hilda the day before. The doll was nowhere to be found.

"Hilda is missing," she told Nina and Jeff.

"So what?" Nina asked.

"You should be happy," Jeff said. "You've been trying to get rid of that doll all week."

That much was true. But now that the doll was missing, Cassidy worried even more. "Where could it be? What is it up to? What if it's like those dolls in the movies Jeff saw? It could be plotting something terrible right now," she told her friends.

"Stop overreacting," Nina said. "Now you can relax."

Nina was wrong. The doll was out of sight, but the ghosts weren't.

The class had barely gotten to work when the air near Cassidy's desk fizzled and popped until Ozzy took shape. He floated on one side of Cassidy. Then he stretched his arm around and tapped her on the other side. When Cassidy looked the wrong way, Ozzy bent over double with laughter. "Gotcha!" he said. The wind from his words sent Cassidy's paper fluttering to the floor. "Look at that," Ozzy said.

When Cassidy looked down, Ozzy poked her in the chin with his finger. At least he tried to. But his finger slid right through Cassidy's chin. "Gotcha again,"

he said. The more he laughed, the easier it was for Cassidy to see him.

"Where did you learn those silly tricks?" Jeff asked later when the rest of the class had filed out for a bathroom break.

"The Internet," Ozzy said. "We got into the computer and surfed at night."

"Don't you mean you got *on* the computer?" Nina asked.

"No," Ozzy said. "We got *into* it. Like this." Ozzy's smile stretched from ear to ear. He started twirling like a tornado until he was long and skinny like a piece of sparkling twine. Then, before the kids could say *boo*, Ozzy slipped through the spot where the Internet cord plugged into the computer. The monitor flickered. It sparkled. It blinked. Images began flashing across the screen so fast it hurt Cassidy's eyes. "Stop," she pleaded. "Before you crash the entire system!"

The computer screen dimmed and then

went dark as Ozzy oozed out of the computer and took shape again.

"Great," Jeff whispered as the rest of the class came back into the room and took their seats. "Just what Ozzy needed to learn on the Internet. Practical jokes."

"We've all been surfing," Ozzy said.

"Not all of us," Becky said. She floated to the right side of Ozzy. "I had better things to do."

"We learned new things," Calliope said as she and Sadie appeared between Cassidy's, Nina's, and Jeff's desks.

"Songs," Sadie moaned. "We learned new songs." Calliope and Sadie started to sing. Calliope sang in a high voice. Sadie's voice was low and mournful. The more they sang, the stronger they seemed to grow. Nate and Ozzy even joined in the singing. "Who let the dogs out? Who? Who?"

After a week of hiding, the ghosts had come out in full force.

Cassidy looked around the room. She was sure everyone else would hear, but the other kids were bent over their desks doing math.

Ghosts were like that. They could choose who could hear and see them. That was good in one way but bad in another. So far the ghosts only let Nina, Jeff, and Cassidy know about them. That meant that while the other kids were getting their work done, Nina, Cassidy, and

Jeff were being distracted by a roomful of partying ghosts.

Even Huxley, the ghost dog, seemed friskier than ever. He really wanted to play fetch. Huxley concentrated extra hard, which is what a ghost needed to do to touch something in the real world. He picked up a wad of paper and carried it back over to Jeff.

Jeff looked to make sure Mr. Morton wasn't watching. Then Jeff flicked the paper wad across the room. Cassidy noticed that the more Huxley fetched, the better at it he became. He wasn't concentrating nearly as hard, but he was still able to grab the paper in his ghost jaws and carry it back to Jeff.

Every ghost was having a blast. Every ghost, that is, except Becky. She hovered in the back of the room with her arms crossed and her bottom lip stuck out. Her face had turned an unhappy shade of gray.

Cassidy took one look at Becky and knew trouble was brewing.

9
Never Go into the Basement Alone!

"We have to find Hilda!" Cassidy hissed to Jeff and Nina. When the rest of the class lined up for art, Cassidy pulled Nina and Jeff to the back of the line.

"Why?" Jeff asked. "I thought you wanted to get rid of Hilda."

"That doll is up to no good," Cassidy said. "I'm sure of it. And I think the rest of the ghosts know it, too. We have to find Hilda before it's too late."

"Maybe the doll disappeared," Nina said. "The ghosts even seem to be back to their normal, bothersome selves."

"I wish Hilda would disappear," Cassidy said. "But I know that doll is around here somewhere. I just know it."

The kids hid in the coatroom until the rest of the class left. Then Cassidy, Jeff, and Nina searched the basement.

Becky swooped in front of them. "You better go with your class," she warned.

Cassidy waved Becky out of the way. "We can't," Cassidy said. "We're looking for something."

Becky swirled in front of Cassidy. "Leave it be," Becky warned, "or you'll be sorry. You'll all be sorry."

"What are you talking about?" Nina asked. But Becky disappeared. The basement classroom was shrouded in silence.

Jeff cupped his hand over his ear and leaned toward the open door that led to the hallway. "Do you hear that?" he asked.

The two girls held their breath so they could listen. Voices. They heard voices.

Jeff tiptoed out into the hallway. Cassidy and Nina followed. They hugged the damp wall as they followed the sound of the voice. It faded in and out, as if someone was pacing back and forth as they talked. The three kids crept down the hallway. Deep shadows swallowed them the farther away they went from the classroom.

"Who could it be?" Jeff whispered into the darkness.

"Is it the ghosts?" Nina asked.

Jeff shook his head. "The ghosts wouldn't bother hiding from us."

"Maybe they're hiding from Hilda," Cassidy said.

"Or maybe it's a new ghost," Nina said with a whimper. "And this ghost might not be so friendly."

"As if the ghosts we already have would win a best-friend-in-the-world trophy," Jeff said with a laugh.

"I'm worried that Hilda has been off getting stronger and making plans to attack us," Cassidy said. Her face was pale and she definitely looked worried.

"This is just like those ghost stories Jeff always talks about," Nina said. "The ones where the kids go down in the basement alone."

Jeff nodded. "I know exactly what you mean. The kids head down the dark steps. The lights flicker, then go out completely. They're surrounded by a darkness that's blacker than black."

"Is it getting darker in here?" Nina asked. "Maybe we should turn back and get a flashlight."

"There's not enough time," Cassidy said. "We have to find Hilda before Mr. Morton realizes we're not with the rest of the class."

"Just like in the movies," Jeff added as the three kids continued into the shadows of the basement. "Nobody realizes the kids are missing as they make their

way closer and closer to whatever is waiting for them. Only, the kids don't know something is there."

Nina's steps were getting slower and slower. Now she stopped. "W . . . wh . . . what's waiting for them?" she asked, her voice squeaking at the end.

Jeff faced his friend. "Do you really want to know?"

Nina nodded, but just barely.

Jeff took a tiny step toward Nina. "It's a great, big, hairy SPIDER!" And then Jeff reached out and grabbed Nina's arm.

If there was one thing Nina hated, it was spiders, and everyone knew it. Nina took a deep breath to scream, but Cassidy slapped her hand over Nina's mouth just in time. "Shh!" Cassidy warned. "We don't want anyone to know we're here."

Nina shook Cassidy's hand away. "We shouldn't be here at all. We know for a fact someone is down there. We can hear them. We need to get out of here before whoever is down there finds us."

"Maybe Nina is right," Jeff said. He was no longer smiling. Now he was as serious as a math test.

Cassidy and Nina stared at Jeff. If Jeff was scared, then it had to be bad.

"Let's get out of here before it's too late," Jeff said.

The three kids turned. All at once. When they did, Cassidy tripped over her shoelace. Nina stumbled against Cassidy. Jeff tripped over them both. They all tumbled into a heap on the cold floor.

The voice from the end of the hallway fell silent, and the basement grew as quiet as a graveyard at midnight. And then the door at the end of the hallway swung open.

The three kids gulped and got ready to face their doom.

10
Nothing but the Facts

Ms. Finkle stepped out of a storage room and glared down at the kids. "Shouldn't you be with the rest of your class?" she asked.

"Um," Cassidy said.

"Errr," Nina added.

"We were looking for pencil sharpener shavings to add to a collage," Jeff said. That was just like Jeff. He was as quick with an excuse as he was with his feet.

Ms. Finkle looked over the top of her glasses at them. Her silver-painted fingernails tapped her chin for a full thirteen seconds. "Olivia is known to save many things," she finally said, "but pencil shavings are not one of them. Now scoot to class!"

The three friends scrambled up from

the floor and hurried up the steps, but not so fast that Cassidy couldn't peek into the storage room. What she saw made her heart skip a beat.

"Who do you think she was talking to?" Jeff asked when they were away from Ms. Finkle.

"I know exactly who she was talking to," Cassidy said. "It was Hilda, the haunted doll. I know because I saw the doll sitting on a chair inside that room."

Nina rolled her eyes. "Principals are way too busy to be playing with dolls."

"Hilda is not an ordinary doll," Cassidy said.

Jeff pulled Nina and Cassidy aside. "Let's consider the facts," he said.

Cassidy nodded and started telling what she knew. "One, that doll keeps moving. Two, when the doll is nearby, the ghosts hide. That means they're scared of it. Three, Becky keeps trying to warn me about something. I know exactly what it is: Hilda. There's something freaky about that doll, and now even Ms. Finkle is acting strange."

Cassidy took a deep breath and counted off on her fingers. "See. It's as easy as one, two, three. That doll is haunting our basement — and it's scaring the ghosts! That's nothing but the facts."

"You don't know that for sure," Nina argued.

"Cassidy doesn't know," Jeff said, "but obviously there is someone who does."

"Who?" Cassidy and Nina asked at the same time.

Jeff pointed back down the basement steps. "The ghosts of Sleepy Hollow, that's who," he said.

Cassidy nodded. "Jeff is right. And there's only one way for us to find out what they know. We have to ask them."

For the rest of the day the kids tried to concentrate on their work, but it was hard. They kept looking over their shoulders, expecting to see the doll peering back at them. Finally, the bell rang, ending the day, and the rest of the class hurried out the door for an afternoon of freedom. Cassidy, Jeff, and Nina hid behind the lost-and-found box and waited until Mr. Morton left the room. Then they tiptoed back into the classroom.

"We need to talk," Cassidy called out to the empty room. "Now."

It wasn't long before the air swirled and sparkled with glitter dust. First, Ozzy appeared. Then Sadie.

"Whyyyyyy?" Sadie moaned. She sounded even sadder than usual. "Are you mad? Pleeeeeeeease don't be mad at meeeeeeeeee."

"No one is mad at you," Cassidy said. "We need information."

"I know just the place where you can find out anything you need to know," Ozzy said with a grin. He flew across the room and landed on top of the computer. Before Cassidy could stop him, Ozzy oozed inside. The computer burped into action. "What do you need to know?" Ozzy asked. It sounded strange hearing his voice come through the computer's speakers.

Cassidy shook her head. "Get out of there," she told him. "There are some things the computer will never have the answers to, and this is one of those things."

"We need to know about Hilda," Nina said.

"Noooooooo," Sadie cried. "Not the dolllllllll."

Sadie's wailing rattled the pictures on the wall. They trembled and shook until Edgar had to leave his place under the tree in the picture. "Stop that crying," Edgar said.

Ozzy flew out of the computer, leaving the screen blank. He tumbled through the air to stand next to Edgar.

"They want to know about Hilllllllllda!" Sadie cried.

Edgar rolled his eyes so far up in his head they completely disappeared. "You can definitely stop wailing about that stuffed piece of nuisance," Edgar said.

"But why does it scare you so much?" Nina wanted to know.

"Is Hilda haunted?" Cassidy asked.

"Is it plotting something terrible?" Jeff wanted to know.

Edgar's eyes rolled back around. "What a great idea for a story," he said, scribbling in his journal. "A haunted doll who tries to destroy a school. I like it!" Edgar oozed back into his picture and settled under the tree. The kids could hear his ghostly pencil scratching across the paper as he wrote.

"You mean, it's only a story?" Nina asked. "The doll isn't haunted?"

"Of course not," Ozzy said.

"Then how did Hilda keep reappearing?" Cassidy asked.

"Oh, that's easy," Calliope said. "We knew Olivia wanted you to have it, so whenever you lost it, we made sure you got it back."

"We were hoping you would take it home so we never had to see it again," Sadie said sadly.

"Then where is it now?" Cassidy asked.

Sadie shook her head. "We thought you finally took it home."

"Not me," Cassidy said.

"Well, good riddance to it wherever it is," Ozzy said. "Dolls are dumb anyway. Especially that doll."

"Why don't you like Hilda?" Nina wanted to know.

"Our teacher made the doll as a gift," Sadie said sadly. "But Miss Hinkleberry did not like the doll at all and she threw it in the basement."

"Who was Miss Hinkleberry?" Nina asked.

"Hilda Hinkleberry was the headmistress of Sleepy Hollow," Edgar told them, looking up from his writing journal. "She had a job very much like your Ms. Finkle."

"Only Miss Hinkleberry was strict and demanding," Sadie explained. "She allowed no dillydallying. We all had to do our best. Becky always wanted to please Miss Hinkleberry."

"When Becky saw the doll in Olivia's hands, she thought it was the ghost of Miss Hinkleberry," Ozzy explained.

"We tried to tell Becky it was just a doll, but she wouldn't believe us," Sadie said.

"Now Becky doesn't want to come out," Ozzy said. "She's afraid Miss Hinkleberry will get mad again, because Becky isn't good at a single thing."

"But Becky is good at a lot of things," Cassidy said.

"She can't read. She can't cipher. She doesn't know her geography," Sadie told Cassidy.

"'Tis true," her brother Ozzy said. "No matter how much I tutored her, Becky just didn't catch on."

Jeff, Cassidy, and Nina were surprised that Ozzy tutored his sister. "I wasn't much of a teacher," Ozzy admitted. "I didn't have the patience."

"Not like Cassidy," Sadie said. "We've been watching her teach Olivia. Cassidy's a good teacher."

"*We* learned about the computers, too," Edgar said. "Thanks to Cassidy."

Nina and Jeff admitted that Cassidy had a lot of patience. "That's what you're good at," Nina told her.

"You're good at figuring things out and then showing other people," Jeff added.

"Maybe you could help Becky," Nina suggested. "You could teach her just like you're teaching Olivia!"

11
Ghost Lessons

"D . . . O . . . G," Becky stuttered. "D-a-wwww-ggg. Dog!"

"That's right!" Cassidy cheered. "You're doing great."

Becky beamed and scooted away from Nina's desk. She danced through the air in the room. Cassidy had been helping Becky learn to read every morning for the last week. Every day, Becky had glowed stronger and brighter.

"Thanks, Cassidy," Becky said as she danced. "I'll always be grateful to you, but what I really want is to learn how to dance."

"You love dancing, don't you?" Cassidy asked as Jeff and Nina walked into the classroom.

"Yes!" Becky said. She did a flip and

landed in Mr. Morton's coffee cup. Yesterday's leftover coffee splashed all over Cassidy. Becky popped her head out of the cup. "Will you teach me?"

Cassidy shrugged. "I don't know anything about dancing."

"I do," Jeff bragged.

"I do, too," Nina said.

"Teach me," Becky begged.

Jeff tapped his toes. He moved his shoulders. He slid his feet across the floor

to an imaginary hip-hop song. "Try this," Jeff said. His sneakers moving across the tile floor made pleasant tapping sounds, but when Becky tried it, there was no sound at all.

Becky frowned. "I can't do it," she moaned.

"Try another kind of dancing," Nina suggested. "This is ballet. I took it in first grade." Nina stood on her toes and walked across the floor. She twirled around and around.

Becky's eyes gleamed. "I like that. Let me do it." Becky tiptoed through Jeff's desk with her arms above her head like Nina had done. Then Becky spun around and around.

"That's great!" Nina cheered, but Becky didn't stop. She kept spinning until she drilled herself through the floor.

"Where did she go?" Cassidy said.

"Maybe she found a new way to China," Jeff said with a laugh.

"This is serious," Nina said. "What if Becky gets lost?"

Nina shouldn't have worried because just then, Becky shot back up through the floor and landed inside a light fixture.

"Are you okay?" Cassidy asked her.

"No," Becky sobbed. The lightbulb shone through her pale skin. "I didn't do the dance right."

"It's okay," Nina told her. "It took me a whole year to learn that. Dancing takes practice."

Becky floated down to the floor. "Really?"

"Sure," Cassidy said. "It's just like reading. You have to keep trying and trying."

"You're exactly right," Nina said, looking at Cassidy. "Everything takes practice. Even volleyball and running relay races."

Cassidy looked at her best friend and knew Nina was right.

"We could help you practice for Field Day," Jeff told Cassidy, "just like you're helping Becky with reading."

"And both you and Jeff are helping me dance," Becky added as she tried hip-hopping across the chalkboard.

Cassidy looked at her friends. Then she looked at Becky as the little ghost slipped from the chalkboard and landed in the trash can by the classroom door.

Cassidy smiled. "I guess you're right," she said. "I can't expect to be good unless I try."

Becky popped out of the trash can like

a cork. Then she flew out of the room. In two seconds she returned with Hilda. "I'm sorry I hid this," Becky confessed. "I didn't want her to see me."

"Thanks," Cassidy said softly and held the doll at arm's length.

"Don't you like it?" Becky asked.

Cassidy started to lie, but then she admitted the truth. "Something about this doll gives me the creeps."

Becky giggled. "I know what you mean. If you want, I'll keep Hilda for you."

"I thought you hated that doll," Nina said to Becky.

Becky smiled and her face turned a pale shade of pink. "I did when I thought it was the real Miss Hinkleberry. But seeing Hilda reminds me of what Miss Hinkleberry used to tell us all the time — that anyone can learn new things. We just have to keep trying."

"You mean, trying things like running in races at Field Day?" Cassidy asked with a little smile of her own.

"Exactly," Nina said with nod. "And you have friends that will help you!"

Becky concentrated very hard so she could take the doll from Cassidy. "I want to learn about everything," she told the kids. "And you are going to help me."

Jeff groaned. "Teaching a classroom of ghosts sounds like more work than study-

ing for a science test. Don't you think so, Cassidy?"

Cassidy didn't answer. She hadn't heard what Jeff said. She was too busy looking at the doll dangling from Becky's pale hands.

Was it Cassidy's imagination, or did the Hilda doll just wink at her?

Ready for more spooky fun?
Then take a sneak peek at the next

Ghostville Elementary®

#8 Ghosts Be Gone!

As the kids lined up at the door to go home that afternoon, they couldn't stop talking about Miss Bogart. Most of the kids in the class still didn't believe in ghosts or ghost hunting. Of course, Nina, Jeff, and Cassidy did. They knew ghosts were real and they knew there were ghosts in their classroom, but they didn't say a word.

"Being a ghost hunter is an awesome idea," Andrew said as their teacher led the kids outside.

"Ghost hunting would be much more exciting than counting money for a bank or writing stories for the newspaper," Andrew added.

"Maybe you could write ghost stories for the newspaper instead," Carla said.

"No way! I'm not going to sit at a desk and type stories into a computer," Andrew told her. "I'm going to sleep all day and spend my nights in haunted houses and cemeteries, hunting ghosts."

"You don't honestly believe Miss Bogart is really a ghost hunter," Darla asked. "Do you?"

Andrew grinned so big the freckles on his cheeks squished together. "Not only do I believe her," he said, "but I'm going to become the youngest and bestest ghost hunter the town of Sleepy Hollow has ever seen. . . ."